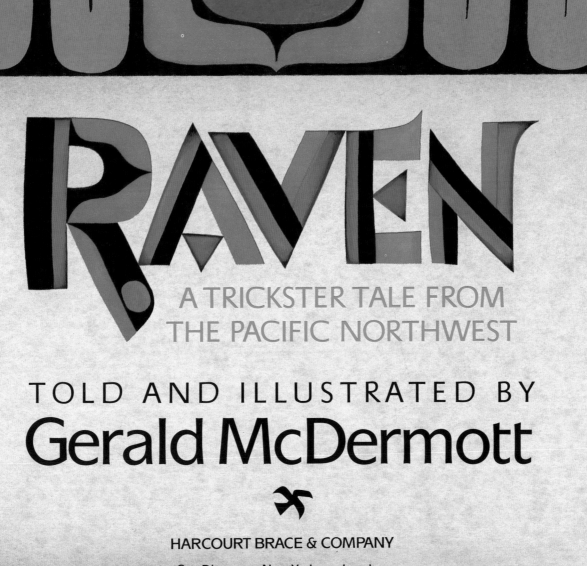

RAVEN

A TRICKSTER TALE FROM THE PACIFIC NORTHWEST

TOLD AND ILLUSTRATED BY
Gerald McDermott

HARCOURT BRACE & COMPANY

San Diego   New York   London

Requests for permission to make copies of any part of the work
should be mailed to Permissions Department,
Harcourt Brace & Company,
8th Floor, Orlando, Florida 32887.

Library of Congress Cataloging-in-Publication Data
McDermott, Gerald.
Raven: a trickster tale from the Pacific Northwest/told and
illustrated by Gerald McDermott. — 1st ed.
p.   cm.
Summary: Raven, a Pacific Coast Indian trickster, sets out to find
the sun.
ISBN 0-15-265661-8
1. Indians of North America — Northwest, Pacific — Legends.
[1. Indians of North America — Northwest, Pacific — Legends.]
I. Title.
E99.N77M33   1993
398.2'089970795 — dc20   91-14563

The paintings in this book were done in gouache, colored pencil,
and pastel on heavyweight cold-press watercolor paper.
The display type was set in Mixage by Central Graphics, San Diego,
California, and in Newtext by Latent Lettering, New York, New York.
The text type was set in Mixage by Central Graphics, San Diego, California.
Color separations by Bright Arts, Ltd., Singapore
Production supervision by Warren Wallerstein and David Hough
Typography designed by Lydia d'Moch

C D E

Printed in Singapore

Along the coast of the Pacific Northwest, as far
north as Alaska, Raven is the central character in
most Native American myths and tales. A shape-
shifter imbued with magical powers, he is at once
brave and cunning, greedy and gluttonous. Raven
is a trickster on a cosmic scale, mischief-maker,
and culture hero, at times wreaking havoc and at
others bestowing on humankind the gift of fire,
light, or food.

To this day Raven is a central figure in the richly
imagined tribal arts of the region. He is depicted,
along with other important animal spirits, in a
highly stylized form on totem poles, carved boxes
and utensils, jewelry, weavings, and baskets.

This tale is told with variations throughout all the
native groups of the northwest coast. Within its
dreamlike setting, Raven balances his heroism and
trickery to bring a blessing to the people.

—G. M.

For Trevor, Erin, and Caitlin

aven came.

All the world was in darkness.
The sky above was in darkness.
The waters below were in darkness.
Men and women lived in the dark and cold.

Raven was sad for them.
He said, "I will search for light."

Raven flew across valleys and across mountains.
He flew along rivers and over lakes. There was
darkness all around.

Then he saw a bit of light far away.
He flew and flew and came closer to the light.
The light was at the edge of the water.

The light came from the house of the Sky Chief, and it was shining.
Raven perched high in a pine tree on the shore.
Raven watched.

He saw a beautiful young girl
emerge from the shining house
and go to the edge of the water.

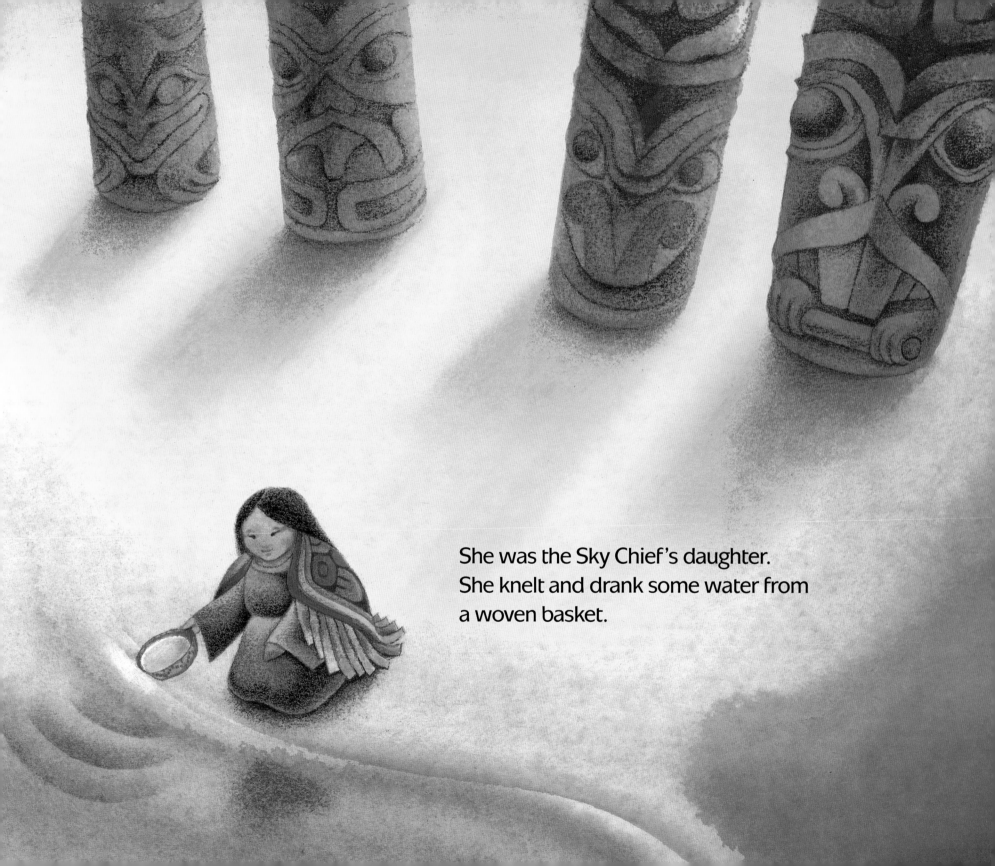

She was the Sky Chief's daughter.
She knelt and drank some water from
a woven basket.

Raven changed himself into a pine needle.

He fell down from the tree and floated on the water.

When the girl drank again, she swallowed the pine needle.

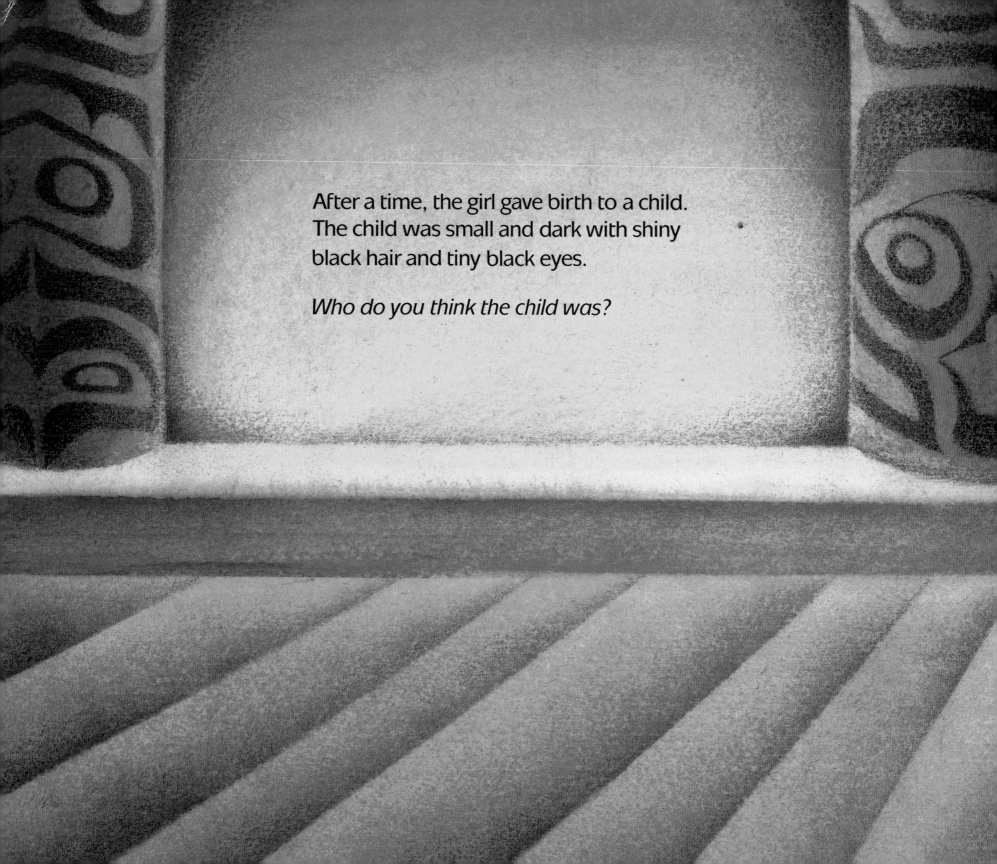

After a time, the girl gave birth to a child.
The child was small and dark with shiny
black hair and tiny black eyes.

Who do you think the child was?

It was Raven.
Raven had been reborn as a boy child.

The Sky Chief was delighted with his daughter's child. He called him grandchild. He played with the boy and carved toys for him. He invited the elders to come and see the curious, wonderful child.

The elders gathered in the shining house
with the Sky Chief and his daughter.
They watched Raven-child crawl
around the floor of the lodge. He
pretended to be playing. All the time,
he was trying to find where the light
was hidden.

He saw a box in the corner
of the lodge.

The box was large.
It was carved and painted
with many colors.
The box was bright. It glowed.
Raven-child said, "Ga! Ga!"

"What do you want?" asked his mother.
Raven-child said, "Ga! Ga!" He began to cry.
"What does the child want?" asked the elders.
Raven-child said, "Ga! Ga!" He cried and cried.
"My grandchild wants the box," said the Sky Chief.

The young woman placed the box in front of Raven-child, but he continued to cry.

She took the lid off the box.
Inside was a smaller box.

She took the lid off that box.
Inside was a smaller box.

His mother took the lid off that box, and light
poured out of it. Light flooded the room.
Inside the box was a shining ball, blazing with light.

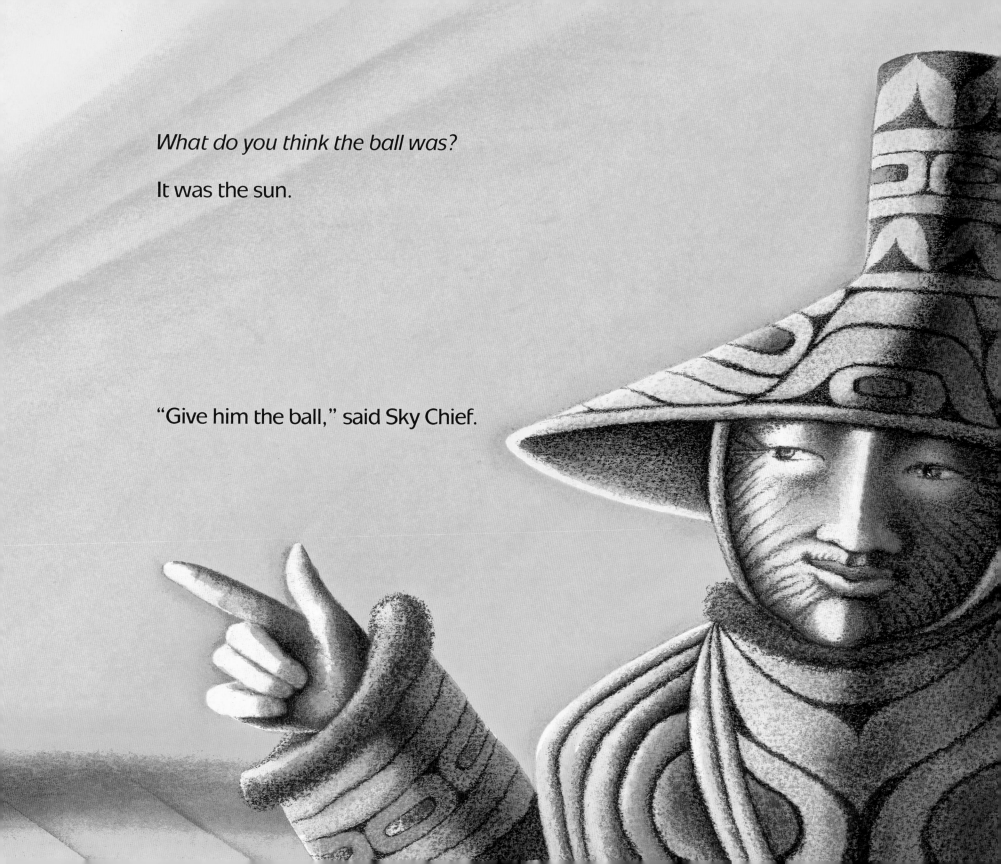

What do you think the ball was?

It was the sun.

"Give him the ball," said Sky Chief.

His mother gave Raven-child the ball.
Raven-child stopped crying.
He began to play with it.
He rolled it around the floor of the lodge.
"Ga! Ga!"

Then he changed into a bird.
"Ha! Ha!"

He became Raven once again.
"Caw! Caw!"

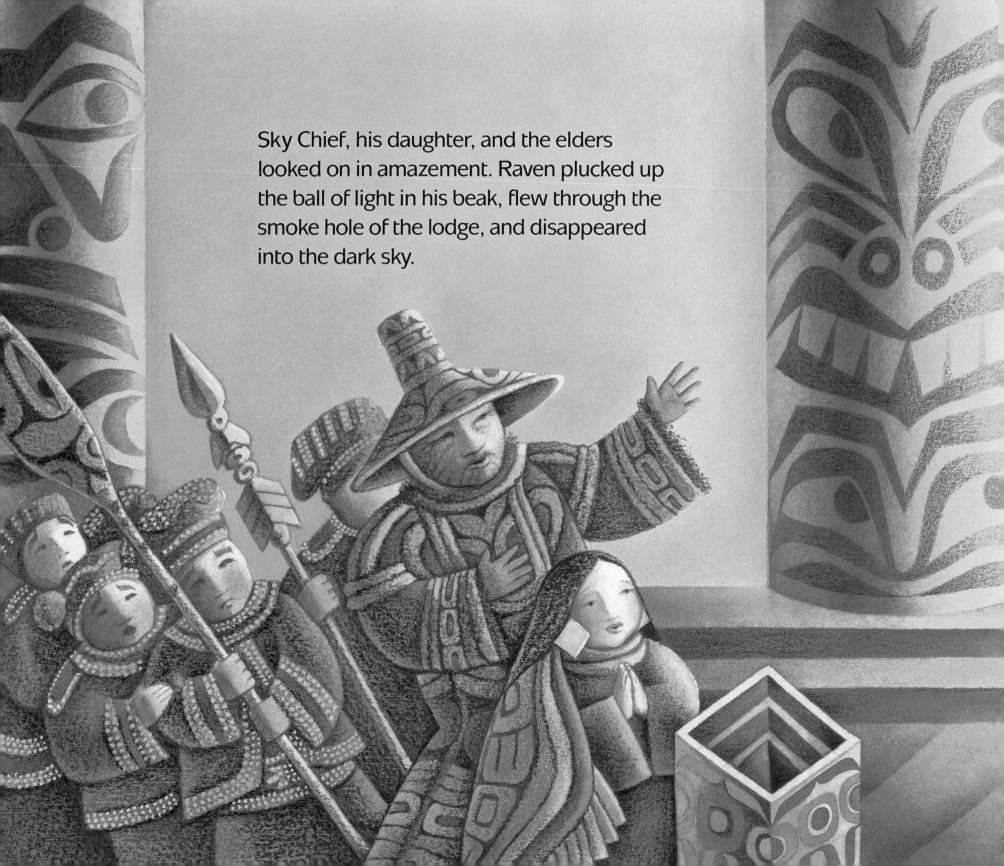

Sky Chief, his daughter, and the elders looked on in amazement. Raven plucked up the ball of light in his beak, flew through the smoke hole of the lodge, and disappeared into the dark sky.

Raven flew over the valleys and the mountains.
He flew along the rivers and across the lakes.

Raven threw the sun high in the sky,
and it stayed there.
This is how Raven stole the sun
and gave it to all the people.

And why do the people always feed Raven?

To thank him for bringing them light.